Allyson Felix

The Fastest Girl for Kids

Victor Lewis

Copyright

All rights reserved. No part of this publication may be reproduced, distributed, or transmitted in any form or by any means, including photocopying, recording, and other electronic or mechanical methods, without prior written permission of the publisher, except in case of briefs quotation embodied in critical reviews and certain other noncommercial uses permitted by copyright law.

Copyright © Victor Lewis,2024

Table of Contents

Table of Contents	3
Introduction	4
Chapter 1: Childhood in Los Angeles: A Girl with a Big Smile and Big Dreams	**13**
Chapter 2: Skipping College for the Olympics: Allyson's Bold Decision	**20**
Overcoming Difficulties and Facing Challenges	27
Chapter 3: The Ultimate Olympian	**36**
Allyson's Training and Nutrition	44
Chapter 4: Life Off the Track	**52**
Giving Back and Inspiring Others	60
Fun Facts About Allyson Felix	**68**
Messages for Young Athletes	**74**
Q&A: Test Your Knowledge	**80**
Conclusion	**85**

Introduction

Meet Allyson Felix: The Queen of the Track

Allyson Felix is a name that resonates not just in the world of track and field, but across the broader landscape of sports and social advocacy. Born on November 18, 1985, in Los Angeles, California, Felix grew up in a family that valued faith, education, and hard work. Her father, Paul, was a pastor and professor, and her mother, Marlean, was a schoolteacher. From a young age, Felix was imbued with a sense of purpose and determination that would serve as the foundation for her remarkable journey.

Felix's athletic talent was evident early on, though she was initially more interested in basketball. However, once she started sprinting in high school, it became clear that she had found her true calling. Despite being nicknamed "Chicken Legs" due to her slender build, Felix was unstoppable on the track. She quickly rose to national prominence, winning state titles and setting records in the 200 meters. By the time she graduated from Los Angeles Baptist High School, Felix had already secured a sponsorship deal with Adidas and was on her way to becoming one of the fastest women in the world.

At just 18 years old, Felix made her Olympic debut at the 2004 Athens Games. Competing against seasoned veterans, she won a silver medal in the 200 meters, signaling the start of what would become an illustrious career. Over the next two decades, Felix would go on to compete in five consecutive Olympic Games, an achievement that few athletes in any sport can claim. Her tally of 11 Olympic medals—7 gold and 4 silver—makes her the most decorated U.S. track and field athlete in Olympic history, surpassing even the legendary Carl Lewis. Felix's Olympic success is mirrored by her dominance at the World Championships, where she earned 19 medals, including 13 golds, further solidifying her status as one of the greatest sprinters of all time.

However, Allyson Felix's story is not just one of medals and records. It's also a story of resilience, advocacy, and breaking barriers. In 2018, Felix faced one of the most challenging periods of her life when she gave birth to her daughter, Camryn, via an emergency C-section at just 32 weeks. The experience opened Felix's eyes to the struggles faced by female athletes who choose to become mothers. Despite her achievements, Felix found herself fighting for basic rights, including protection from financial penalties due to pregnancy—a situation that sparked widespread outrage when it came to light.

Rather than stay silent, Felix took a stand. In a powerful op-ed for *The New York Times*, she publicly criticized Nike, her longtime sponsor, for its treatment of pregnant athletes. Her courage and willingness to speak out led to significant changes in how companies like Nike support their athletes during pregnancy and postpartum recovery. Felix's advocacy didn't stop there; she went on to partner with Athleta, becoming the first sponsored athlete for the women-focused brand. She also launched her own footwear company, Saysh, which is dedicated to creating shoes designed specifically for women, by women.

Felix's impact extends far beyond the track. She has become a powerful voice for gender equality, racial justice, and maternal health. Her work has inspired countless other athletes to speak out and demand better treatment, and she has used her platform to raise awareness about issues that matter not just in sports, but in society as a whole. Felix's ability to balance her career, motherhood, and activism is a testament to her strength, character, and determination.

In 2021, at the Tokyo Olympics, Felix added two more medals to her collection—a bronze in the 400 meters and a gold in the 4x400 meter relay—bringing her Olympic total to 11. This achievement was particularly meaningful, as it came after years of overcoming the challenges of motherhood, advocating for change, and competing at the highest level well into her 30s. Felix's ability to compete and win on the world's biggest stage, even after nearly two decades in the sport, is a testament to her extraordinary talent, resilience, and work ethic.

Allyson Felix's legacy is far-reaching and multifaceted. She will be remembered not only as one of the greatest sprinters in history but also as a trailblazer who used her voice and influence to make the world a better place. Her journey from a young girl with "chicken legs" to a global icon of strength, courage, and integrity serves as an inspiration to millions. Whether on the track, in the boardroom, or on the front lines of social justice, Felix has shown that with passion, determination, and a willingness to stand up for what is right, anything is possible.

Chapter 1: Childhood in Los Angeles: A Girl with a Big Smile and Big Dreams

Allyson Felix's journey to becoming one of the greatest track and field athletes of all time began in the sunny streets of Los Angeles, California. Born on November 18, 1985, she grew up in a close-knit family that valued faith, education, and hard work. Her father, Paul, was a pastor and professor of New Testament at The Master's Seminary, and her mother, Marlean, was an elementary school teacher. Felix was the younger of two children, and from an early age, she looked up to her older brother, Wes, who was also a talented sprinter.

As a child, Allyson was known for her big smile and her boundless energy. She was the type of kid who couldn't sit still for long, always eager to run, jump, and play. Despite her eventual rise to athletic stardom, Allyson's childhood was surprisingly ordinary in many ways. She loved playing outside with her friends, riding her bike around the neighborhood, and playing basketball—a sport she initially preferred over running. With her slim frame and long legs, no one could have predicted that this cheerful, playful girl would one day become one of the fastest women on the planet.

Growing up, Allyson attended Los Angeles Baptist High School, where her natural athleticism began to shine. It wasn't until her freshman year that she discovered her talent for sprinting. Encouraged by her brother, Wes, who had become a standout sprinter himself, Allyson decided to try out for the track team. Though she had always been fast, her success on the track took everyone by surprise—including herself.

Despite her unassuming, slender build, Allyson quickly earned the nickname "Chicken Legs" among her peers, a playful reference to her long, lean legs. But those "chicken legs" were powerful, and they carried her to victory after victory on the track. Her speed was undeniable, and soon, it became clear that Allyson Felix was no ordinary sprinter.

By her junior year, Allyson had become a dominant force in high school track and field. She won state titles, set records, and caught the attention of college scouts and professional sponsors. Even as her success on the track grew, Allyson remained grounded. She was a dedicated student, balancing her athletic pursuits with her schoolwork and never losing sight of the values her parents had instilled in her.

Despite her rising fame, Allyson was still just a teenager with big dreams. She dreamed of competing on the world's biggest stages, representing her country at the Olympics, and becoming the best sprinter she could be. Her big smile and infectious positivity endeared her to everyone who knew her, and her work ethic and determination set her apart from her peers.

As Allyson prepared to graduate from high school, she faced a life-changing decision: whether to accept a college scholarship or to go pro right out of high school. Ultimately, she decided to sign with Adidas and embark on a professional career, a bold move for someone so young. But for Allyson Felix, this was just the beginning of a journey that would see her achieve greatness on the track, advocate for change off the track, and inspire millions around the world.

Her childhood in Los Angeles—filled with love, faith, and the freedom to dream big—provided the perfect foundation for the extraordinary life that was to come.

Chapter 2: Skipping College for the Olympics: Allyson's Bold Decision

Allyson Felix found herself at a crossroads as she neared the end of her high school career—a point many young athletes must make one of the most important decisions of their lives. Following a remarkable high school track career at Los Angeles Baptist High School, where she broke records and attracted national attention, Allyson had drawn the attention of college recruiters all around. From prominent colleges, offers arrived, each promising to help her academic and athletic growth.

Many athletes find that the road to excellence passes through university hallways, where they can refine their abilities, graduate, and become ready for a career in professional sports. For Allyson, though, the conventional path seemed to be inappropriate. She dreamed of representing her nation on the largest platform in the world, the Olympic Games, dreams of which could not wait. Her heart was already set on following those Olympic goals, even as much as she appreciated education and knew the value of college.

Just eighteen years old, Allyson made a daring choice that would turn her life around: she decided to leave college and sign a sponsorship contract with Adidas. Many found this action startling. She was still a teenager, just out of high school, and entering a world predominated by seasoned athletes with years of experience. Allyson, however, was a genius with the talent, determination, and maturity needed to compete at the highest level—not just an average teenager.

Making the choice wasn't simple. Allyson saw the value of a college degree and was quite dedicated to her study. Still, the chance to train full-time and challenge the greatest in the world was too great to miss. She understood postponing her Olympic aspirations would mean missing her prime years as a sprinter. Allyson jumped with family support, who believed in her ability and trusted her decision.

Being professional meant Allyson would be forfeiting the usual college experience—no dorm life, no college track meetings, and no wandering across campus with other students. Rather, she entered a world of rigorous training, global competitiveness, and great expectations. Allyson, meanwhile, was ready. Working nonstop with her coaches, she concentrated on the 200 meters—the event where she had already proved her ability to compete with the best.

Her choice was soon confirmed when she just months from going professional qualified for the 2004 Athens Olympics. Allyson, then eighteen, entered the Olympic arena representing the United States alongside the fastest women in the world. Though the strain was great, Allyson managed it with the grace of a seasoned performer. She competed for a silver medal in the 200-meter final, just missing gold but declaring her entrance on the world scene.

An amazing feat, winning an Olympic silver medal at such a young age signaled the start of a famous career. Few could have predicted, but Allyson's audacious choice to forgo college paid out in ways that With a career spanning five Olympic Games and an 11 medal count—including 7 golds—it placed her on a road to becoming among the most decorated athletes in Olympic history.

Allyson never overlooked, though, the value of education. She would later on in her career obtain her college degree, demonstrating that it's never too late to reach your academic ambitions even after you've mastered the realm of athletics.

Allyson, Thought it was a chance, Felix's decision to skip college for the Olympics was one she was ready for. Her confidence, vision, and unwavering dedication to her objectives are evident in her courageous action at such a young age. It reminds us that occasionally the road to success is not necessarily the traditional one and that with skill, will, and the correct support remarkable things are possible.

Overcoming Difficulties and Facing Challenges

Allyson. Felix's path to rank among the most decorated track & field athletes in history was hardly flawless. She encountered several difficulties and roadblocks over her career—on and off the course—that tried her fortitude, will, and moral strength of character. Still, Felix showed time and again that she could withstand hardship, rising each time stronger and more resolved.

Felix's first obstacle was the pressure of walking onto the world scene at a very young age. She found herself vying against some of the world's top athletes, many of whom were far older and more experienced, after electing to turn professional right out of high school and skip college. It was intimidating to go from being a high school standout to competing in the Olympics at barely eighteen years old. She might have been overwhelmed by the weight of expectations and the intensity of the competition, but Felix answered the call. Her silver medal in the 200 meters at the 2004 Athens Olympics spoke to her capacity for under-pressure performance.

Felix's career developed, and she had to contend with the physical and psychological pressures of preserving optimal performance over several years. Felix excelled in several disciplines—100 meters, 200 meters, 400 meters, and several relays—each demanding distinct training and techniques, unlike some competitors who might concentrate on one event. Her body suffered from juggling numerous activities; she had to control injuries, weariness, and the natural wear and tear of years of fierce competition. Felix kept pushing her boundaries despite these obstacles; she regularly performed at the top level and took medals at several Olympic Games and World Championships.

Felix's most important challenge occurred in 2018 when she developed problems during her pregnancy. Born prematurely by an emergency C-section at barely 32 weeks, Felix's daughter Camryn Felix's health and the health of her child were gravely in jeopardy throughout the horrific and life-changing event. Felix also faced the hard reality of being a female athlete negotiating pregnancy and parenthood in a rigorous career as she healed from the operation and adjusted to life as a new mother.

Felix had another obstacle at this time that would propel her front and center in a more general debate about women's rights and equity in sports. Felix's longtime sponsor, Nike, suggested drastically cutting her contract after delivery, noting her poor performance both during and following pregnancy. Felix, who had always been known for her quiet resolve, felt she should speak out at this point.

Felix questioned the lack of support from sponsors and revealed the difficulties female athletes have juggling their careers with parenting in a potent op-ed written in *The New York Times*.

Felix's campaigning resulted in public backlash and Nike changed their rules to guarantee that female athletes would not be financially punished for starting families. An amazing act of bravery and leadership, her readiness to defend herself—and all women—during one of the most sensitive periods of her life was Felix not only overcome the emotional and physical obstacles of her pregnancy, but she also contributed to bringing about significant change in the sports industry so opening the path for next generations of female athletes.

Felix partnered with Athleta, a women-oriented brand that fit her principles after making the tough choice to quit Nike in 2019. She also started Saysh, her own shoe company, created by women for women, therefore proving her dedication to empowering others.

Felix came back to the track better than ever despite both personal and professional obstacles. Her total is now 11

Olympic medals, the most by any U.S. track and field athlete—two more medals—a bronze in the 400 meters and a gold in the 4x400 meter relay—earned at the 2020 Tokyo Olympics (held in 2021 due to the epidemic). Competing at such a high level following all she had been through was simply amazing.

Allyson is Felix's narrative is one of tenacity, fortitude, and the need for self-belief. She has surmounted great obstacles—pressure, injuries, parenthood, and advocacy for equity—each time with grace and will. Her legacy goes beyond only the medals she has earned to include the obstacles she has cleared and the motivation she has given women and athletes all across. Felix has demonstrated that real strength is not only in conquering challenges life presents but also in harnessing those experiences to have a long-lasting effect on the world. Felix has won races.

Chapter 3 The Ultimate Olympian

Allyson Felix's illustrious career has earned her the title of "The Ultimate Olympian," a designation that reflects not just her remarkable achievements on the track, but also her enduring legacy as a trailblazer and role model. Competing in five consecutive Olympic Games from 2004 to 2021, Felix has become the most decorated U.S. track and field athlete in Olympic history, surpassing legends like Carl Lewis. But Felix's status as the ultimate Olympian is about more than the 11 medals—7 gold, 3 silver, and 1 bronze—she's accumulated over nearly two decades of competition. It's about her extraordinary consistency, her ability to adapt and excel in multiple events, and the grace and determination with which she has faced every challenge.

From the moment she stepped onto the Olympic stage as an 18-year-old in Athens, Felix demonstrated a maturity and composure beyond her years. Winning a silver medal in the 200 meters at her first Olympics set the tone for a career that would be defined by excellence and resilience. Felix quickly established herself as a force to be reckoned with in the 200 meters, an event in which she would win three Olympic medals, including gold in 2012 at the London Games. Her performance in London was particularly special, as it was the culmination of years of hard work and the realization of a goal she had been chasing since her first Olympic silver.

But what truly sets Felix apart as the ultimate Olympian is her versatility. Unlike many sprinters who specialize in a single distance, Felix excelled across multiple events, showcasing her incredible range. In addition to her dominance in the 200 meters, Felix became a powerhouse in the 400 meters, an event that requires a unique blend of speed, endurance, and mental toughness. Her gold medal in the 4x400 meter relay at the Beijing Olympics in 2008 marked the beginning of a relay legacy that would see Felix anchor the U.S. team to victory in three consecutive Olympics—Beijing, London, and Rio. These relay victories not only added to her medal count but also highlighted her ability to perform under pressure and her dedication to teamwork.

Felix's career is also defined by her ability to persevere through adversity. The 2016 Rio Olympics were a particularly poignant example of this. Despite being one of the favorites in the 400 meters, Felix was edged out of gold by Shaunae Miller-Uibo of the Bahamas in a dramatic finish where Miller-Uibo dove across the line to win. Felix took silver, but instead of letting the disappointment overshadow her achievements, she returned to the track just days later to lead the U.S. relay team to gold in the 4x400 meters. Her performance in Rio solidified her reputation as an athlete who embodies both grace and grit, someone who could bounce back from setbacks with remarkable resilience.

Perhaps the most remarkable chapter in Felix's Olympic career came at the Tokyo Games in 2021, where she competed as a mother and an advocate for women's rights. After giving birth to her daughter, Camryn, in 2018 and facing the challenges of postpartum recovery, many wondered if Felix could return to the top of her game. But in true Felix fashion, she silenced the doubters with a bronze medal in the 400 meters and a gold in the 4x400 meter relay, bringing her Olympic medal tally to 11. These victories were particularly meaningful, as they symbolized not just athletic triumph, but personal victory over the challenges she had faced as a mother and a vocal advocate for change in the sports world.

Beyond her athletic achievements, Felix's impact as the ultimate Olympian extends to her work off the track. Her advocacy for female athletes, particularly around issues of maternity and sponsorship, has led to significant changes in how companies support women in sports. By speaking out against inequities and using her platform to champion the rights of women and mothers, Felix has left an indelible mark on the world of athletics, inspiring countless others to follow in her footsteps.

Allyson Felix's legacy as the ultimate Olympian is a testament to her extraordinary talent, her unwavering commitment to excellence, and her ability to inspire others through her actions both on and off the track. She has not only redefined what it means to be a champion but has also shown the world that true greatness is measured not just by medals, but by the impact one has on others and the courage to stand up for what is right. As the ultimate Olympian, Felix's story will continue to inspire generations of athletes to come, reminding them that with hard work, resilience, and a commitment to making a difference, anything is possible.

Allyson's Training and Nutrition

Allyson Felix's remarkable success on the track is deeply rooted in her meticulous approach to both training and nutrition. Her journey to becoming one of the greatest sprinters in history involved a rigorous and carefully crafted training routine that balanced speed, strength, and endurance. Felix's workouts included a variety of sprint drills designed to enhance her explosive speed and improve her acceleration. She regularly practiced short sprints ranging from 30 to 200 meters, focusing on maintaining top speed and refining her technique. To simulate the demands of a race, she often did multiple sets with rest intervals, allowing her to push her limits and sharpen her skills. For the 400 meters, endurance training was a crucial part of her routine. Felix incorporated longer runs and interval training to build stamina, enabling her to maintain her speed throughout the entire race. These workouts typically involved running 300 or 400-meter intervals at a slightly reduced pace, with shorter recovery periods to challenge her aerobic capacity and ensure she could finish strong.

Strength training was another vital component of Felix's regimen. She engaged in weightlifting, plyometrics, and bodyweight exercises to build muscle strength, particularly in her legs, core, and upper body. Exercises like squats, deadlifts, lunges, and box jumps helped increase her power and explosiveness, which were essential for her sprinting success. Additionally, core exercises like planks and Russian twists improved her stability and balance, allowing her to maintain optimal form throughout her races. Flexibility and recovery were also key elements of Felix's training. She incorporated stretching, yoga, and foam rolling into her routine to improve flexibility and prevent injuries. Recovery techniques such as ice baths, massages, and adequate rest were prioritized to ensure her body was prepared for the demands of both training and competition. These recovery practices became increasingly important as Felix aged, helping her to extend her career and continue performing at an elite level.

Felix's nutrition played an equally important role in her success. She maintained a balanced diet centered around whole, nutrient-dense foods, providing the energy and nutrients needed to fuel her intense workouts and maintain peak physical condition. Carbohydrates were a primary energy source for her, particularly before training sessions and competitions. Felix opted for complex carbs like whole grains, sweet potatoes, and brown rice, which provided sustained energy. Protein was crucial for muscle recovery and repair, so she included lean sources such as chicken, fish, eggs, and plant-based proteins in her diet. Healthy fats from avocados, nuts, seeds, and olive oil were also important for overall health and energy balance. Before workouts or competitions, Felix focused on consuming easily digestible foods that provided quick energy without weighing her down. A typical pre-workout meal might include oatmeal with fruit and nuts or a smoothie made with bananas, spinach, and protein powder. This ensured she had the energy needed to perform at her best.

Post-workout, Felix prioritized replenishing glycogen stores and repairing muscle tissue. Her meals typically included a mix of protein and carbohydrates, such as grilled chicken with quinoa and vegetables, or a protein shake with a piece of fruit. She also paid close attention to hydration, drinking plenty of water and occasionally including electrolyte-rich beverages to replace what was lost during intense workouts. While Felix primarily focused on getting nutrients from whole foods, she occasionally used supplements to support her diet, especially during periods of intense training. These supplements might include protein powders or vitamins, ensuring she met her nutritional needs even during the most demanding phases of her career.

Through her disciplined approach to training and nutrition, Allyson Felix was able to sustain a long and successful career, consistently performing at the highest levels of track and field. Her commitment to every aspect of her preparation, both on and off the track, is a testament to her dedication to excellence and her relentless pursuit of greatness.

Chapter 4:Life Off the Track

Off the track, Allyson Felix's life is as remarkable as her athletic career. While she has been known globally as a sprinter with unmatched speed and resilience, Felix has also built a life full of purpose, advocacy, and family that goes far beyond her achievements in sports.

One of the most defining aspects of Felix's life off the track is her role as a mother. In 2018, she gave birth to her daughter, Camryn, under challenging circumstances. Camryn was born prematurely via an emergency C-section at just 32 weeks, a situation that put both Felix's and her baby's health at risk. The experience of becoming a mother was life-changing for Felix, not only because of the physical demands of recovering from such a serious procedure but also because of the emotional journey that came with balancing motherhood and her career. Despite the difficulties, Felix embraced her new role with the same determination that she brought to the track. Her daughter became a central focus in her life, and Felix often speaks about the joy and perspective that motherhood has given her. She is open about the challenges of being a working mother, particularly in a demanding field like professional sports, and she has become a vocal advocate for maternal health and the rights of female athletes who are also mothers.

Felix's experience with pregnancy and motherhood also fueled her passion for advocacy. After giving birth, she publicly challenged Nike, her longtime sponsor, over its treatment of pregnant athletes. When Nike proposed significantly reducing her contract after her pregnancy, Felix decided to speak out, writing a powerful op-ed in *The New York Times*. Her actions sparked a larger conversation about the rights of female athletes, particularly around issues of maternity and sponsorship. Felix's advocacy led to significant changes in how companies like Nike support their athletes, ensuring that women are not financially penalized for becoming mothers. This moment marked a turning point not only in Felix's life but also in the sports industry, highlighting the importance of equity and support for women at all stages of their careers.

Felix's commitment to making a difference extends beyond her advocacy work. In 2019, she signed with Athleta, a women-focused brand, becoming their first sponsored athlete. This partnership allowed her to align more closely with her values and continue advocating for women in sports. Felix also ventured into entrepreneurship, launching her own footwear company, Saysh, designed by women, for women. The brand represents more than just shoes—it's a statement about empowerment, inclusivity, and the need for products that cater specifically to women's needs. Through Saysh, Felix has shown that her influence goes beyond athletics; she is a trailblazer in the business world, using her platform to create meaningful change.

The family has always been central to Felix's life. She comes from a close-knit family, and her relationships with her parents and brother have been a source of strength and support throughout her career. Despite her global fame, Felix has remained grounded, often attributing her success to the values instilled in her by her family. Her father, Paul, a pastor and professor, and her mother, Marlean, an elementary school teacher, taught her the importance of faith, education, and perseverance—lessons that have guided her through the highs and lows of her career.

Felix is also dedicated to giving back to the community. She is involved in various charitable initiatives, particularly those focused on youth and education. Through her work, she aims to inspire the next generation to dream big and pursue their goals with determination and integrity. Whether through mentoring young athletes or supporting educational programs, Felix's impact off the track is as profound as her accomplishments on it.

Even with all her achievements, Felix continues to stay connected to the sport she loves. She remains a mentor and role model for up-and-coming athletes, offering guidance and sharing her experiences with those who aspire to follow in her footsteps. Her presence in the world of track and field is still felt, not just as a competitor but as a leader and advocate for positive change.

In her life off the track, Allyson Felix has shown that true greatness is not just about winning medals but about using one's platform to make a difference in the world. Through her roles as a mother, advocate, entrepreneur, and mentor, Felix has built a legacy that transcends athletics, inspiring others to pursue their dreams while standing up for what they believe in. Her story is a testament to the power of resilience, the importance of family, and the impact one person can have on the world around them.

Giving Back and Inspiring Others

Allyson Felix has always recognized the importance of using her platform to give back and inspire others, especially those who look up to her as a role model. Throughout her career, she has been deeply committed to making a positive impact beyond the track, dedicating herself to causes that uplift communities and empower the next generation.

One of the key areas where Felix has made a significant impact is in her work with youth. She understands the power of sports to change lives, just as it did for her. To that end, Felix has been involved in numerous initiatives aimed at supporting young athletes, particularly those from underprivileged backgrounds. She has partnered with various organizations to provide resources, mentorship, and opportunities to kids who might not otherwise have access to the support they need to succeed. Felix often speaks at schools, youth centers, and events, sharing her story and encouraging young people to pursue their dreams, no matter the obstacles they may face.

Felix's passion for education is another driving force behind her philanthropic efforts. She is a strong advocate for ensuring that young people have access to quality education, which she believes is the foundation for a successful and fulfilling life. Felix has supported educational programs that provide scholarships, tutoring, and resources to students in need, helping to remove barriers to learning and opening doors to new opportunities. Her involvement in these programs is not just about giving financial support; she actively engages with students, offering advice and encouragement, and showing them that they too can achieve great things.

In addition to her work with youth and education, Felix has been a powerful advocate for women's rights, particularly in the areas of maternal health and equity in sports. Her personal experiences as a mother and the challenges she faced during and after her pregnancy have fueled her commitment to making sure that other female athletes do not have to face the same struggles. By speaking out against unfair practices and pushing for change, Felix has helped to reshape the conversation around how women are treated in sports, especially when it comes to pregnancy and motherhood. Her efforts have led to significant changes in how sponsors and organizations support female athletes, ensuring that women are not penalized for starting families.

Felix's commitment to giving back extends to her work with her own company, Saysh, which she founded to create footwear designed specifically for women. Through Saysh, Felix is not only addressing a gap in the market but also empowering women to take control of their athletic journeys. The brand is built on principles of inclusivity and female empowerment, reflecting Felix's broader mission to uplift and inspire women everywhere.

Felix's impact as a philanthropist and advocate is amplified by her genuine desire to connect with and uplift others. She is known for her humility and her willingness to engage with people from all walks of life. Whether she's mentoring young athletes, advocating for policy changes, or sharing her experiences with the world, Felix approaches everything she does with a deep sense of responsibility and a commitment to making a difference.

Her work has inspired countless individuals to pursue their dreams and to stand up for what they believe in. Felix has shown that true leadership is about more than just personal success; it's about using that success to create opportunities for others and to drive positive change in the world. She continues to be a beacon of hope and inspiration, demonstrating through her actions that it's possible to achieve greatness while also lifting others along the way.

Allyson Felix's legacy as an athlete is matched by her legacy as a giver and an advocate. She has dedicated herself to causes that matter, making a lasting impact on the lives of countless individuals and helping to pave the way for a more equitable and just world. Her commitment to giving back and inspiring others will continue to influence and motivate generations to come.

Fun Facts About Allyson Felix

Sure! Here are some fun (and funny) facts about Allyson Felix:

1. Chicken Legs to Lightning Speed: As a high schooler, Allyson was nicknamed "Chicken Legs" because of her long, slim legs. But those "chicken legs" turned out to be turbocharged—so fast that if you blinked, you'd miss her crossing the finish line!

2. Late Bloomer in Sneakers: Allyson didn't start running track until her

freshman year of high school. Before that, she was more into basketball. But when she realized she could outrun everyone on the court, she decided to give the track a try. Good decision, right?

3. Olympic Collection: With 11 Olympic medals, Allyson probably has more bling than most jewelry stores. She's practically running out of room in her trophy case—maybe it's time to invest in a medal organizer!

4. Speedy Genes: Running fast might just run in the family. Allyson's brother, Wes, was also a sprinter, and her dad was an

athlete too. If there were a Felix family relay race, you'd want to watch from the sidelines—they'd lap you before you could say "Go!"

5. World Traveler: Thanks to track and field, Allyson has probably visited more countries than most people have stamps on their passports. She's a globe-trotter in spikes, racing her way around the world, one gold medal at a time.

6. Shoe Game Strong: Allyson loves shoes—so much so that she started her footwear brand, Saysh. Now, not only can she run faster than you, but she can do it in

the shoes she designed herself. That's a whole new level of style and speed!

7. Anything Boys Can Do…: In middle school, Allyson raced against the boys in gym class and beat them. No wonder she grew up to be an Olympic champion. Sorry, boys—sometimes, girls just do it better!

8. Multi-Tasking Mom: Allyson doesn't just run fast; she does it while balancing life as a mom. She's a Superwoman, except her cape is a racing bib and her superpower is winning medals and making breakfast at the same time.

9. Advocate Extraordinaire: When she's not busy training, competing, or being a mom, Allyson is out there changing the world. She took on Nike and won—not in a race, but in a battle for maternity rights. Next up, world domination?

10. Running for the Win, Even at 32 Weeks: Allyson might have given birth at 32 weeks, but she's been running life's marathon ever since. Her baby might be the only one in the world who can say, "Yeah, I was already competing in the Olympics from the womb."

11. Olympic Fashionista: Over the years, Allyson has probably worn more racing kits than most people have outfits. She could start her Olympic-themed fashion line—running shoes optional!

12. Forever Young: Despite being in the sport for nearly two decades, Allyson still looks like she could be a college athlete. Maybe all that sprinting is the real fountain of youth?

Allyson Felix isn't just fast—she's fierce, funny, and fabulous. Whether she's racing on the track, advocating for change, or designing shoes, she does it all with a smile and a speed that's hard to match!

Messages for Young Athletes

Here are some motivational and encouraging messages for young athletes, inspired by Allyson Felix:

1. "Believe in your journey, even if it doesn't start the way you expect." Allyson didn't start running track until high school, but once she found her passion, she gave it everything she had. It's never too late to

discover your talent and pursue your dreams.

2. "Let your challenges fuel your fire." Allyson faced many obstacles, from injuries to fighting for women's rights in sports. Instead of letting them stop her, she used those challenges as motivation to keep going and make a difference. You can do the same—turn every setback into a comeback.

3. "Stay true to who you are." Allyson has always been grounded in her values, whether she's on the track or advocating

for change. Be proud of who you are and let that guide you in everything you do.

4. "Dream big, work hard, and don't be afraid to stand up for what's right." Allyson's career is a testament to the power of big dreams and an even bigger work ethic. But it's also about having the courage to speak out when something isn't right. You can be both a champion and a change-maker.

5. "Success isn't just about winning—it's about lifting others." Allyson's greatest victories include her advocacy for women's rights and mentoring younger

athletes. Remember, your success is even greater when you help others along the way.

6. "Embrace your uniqueness." Whether it's being the fastest kid in school or the only girl on the field, your differences make you special. Allyson turned her unique talents into a legendary career—celebrate what makes you, you!

7. "Balance is key." Allyson manages to be a world-class athlete, a mom, and an advocate. Whatever you're passionate about, remember to balance your time, your energy, and your priorities.

8. "Never stop learning and growing." Even after winning multiple Olympic medals, Allyson continues to push herself, learn new things, and strive for improvement. Keep an open mind and always look for ways to grow.

9. "It's okay to rewrite your story." Allyson showed that you can change the narrative, whether it's coming back stronger after an injury or fighting for a new cause. Your journey is yours to write, so don't be afraid to take control of it.

10. Enjoy the process, not just the finish line." Allyson's journey wasn't just about the medals—it was about the lessons learned, the people met, and the impact made along the way. Remember to enjoy every step of your journey, not just the final destination.

Whether you're just starting out or already on your way, remember that every champion was once a beginner. Keep pushing, keep believing, and most importantly, keep having fun!

Q&A: Test Your Knowledge

Here's a fun Q&A quiz to test your knowledge about Allyson Felix!

1. What nickname did Allyson Felix earn in high school due to her slim build?
   a) Speedy
   b) Lightning
   c) Chicken Legs
   d) Track Queen

2. How old was Allyson Felix when she competed in her first Olympics?
   a) 16

b) 18

c) 20

d) 22

3. How many Olympic medals has Allyson Felix won?

   a) 7

   b) 9

   c) 11

   d) 13

4. What major decision did Allyson Felix make right after high school?

   a) To become a basketball player

   b) To turn professional and skip college

   c) To study abroad

d) To take a year off from sports

5. Which shoe company did Allyson Felix challenge over its treatment of pregnant athletes?

   a) Adidas
   b) Puma
   c) Nike
   d) Reebok

6. What is the name of Allyson Felix's footwear brand?

   a) Stride
   b) RunHer
   c) FlyGirl
   d) Saysh

7. Allyson Felix won her first Olympic gold medal in which event?

   a) 100 meters

   b) 200 meters

   c) 400 meters

   d) 4x400 meter relay

8. How many Olympic Games have Allyson Felix competed in?

   a) 3

   b) 4

   c) 5

   d) 6

9. What cause has Allyson Felix become a vocal advocate for, particularly after becoming a mother?

   a) Climate change

   b) Women's rights and maternal health

   c) Education reform

   d) Animal rights

10. Which Olympic Games did Allyson Felix make history by winning her 11th medal, making her the most decorated U.S. track and field athlete?

   a) Beijing 2008

   b) London 2012

   c) Rio 2016

   d) Tokyo 2020

Conclusion

Allyson Felix's journey from a young girl with "chicken legs" sprinting through the streets of Los Angeles to becoming the most decorated U.S. track and field athlete in Olympic history is a testament to her extraordinary talent, resilience, and unwavering dedication. Over nearly two decades, Felix has not only set records and won medals, but she has also redefined what it means to be a champion—both on and off the track.

Her decision to skip college and turn professional right out of high school was the first of many bold moves that would come to characterize her career. At just 18 years old, Felix faced the pressures of the global stage at the 2004 Athens Olympics, where she won her first Olympic silver medal in the 200 meters. This achievement set the tone for what would become one of the most storied careers in the history of athletics. Over the years, Felix's versatility as a sprinter allowed her to dominate in multiple events, from the 100 meters to the 400 meters, and her ability to perform under pressure made her a cornerstone of the U.S. relay teams, leading them to gold on multiple occasions.

But Allyson Felix's legacy extends far beyond her medal count. Throughout her career, she has faced numerous challenges, from the physical demands of maintaining peak performance to the personal challenges of balancing motherhood with elite competition. Perhaps one of the most significant obstacles she encountered was during her pregnancy in 2018 when she underwent an emergency C-section at 32 weeks to deliver her daughter, Camryn. This experience profoundly changed Felix, inspiring her to become a vocal advocate for maternal health and the rights of female athletes.

Felix's courage to speak out against Nike's treatment of pregnant athletes marked a turning point not only in her life but in the broader conversation about women's rights in sports. By sharing her story and challenging one of the biggest names in the industry, Felix brought attention to the inequities faced by women in sports and helped drive meaningful change. Her advocacy led to improved policies that protect female athletes during pregnancy and postpartum recovery, ensuring that they are not financially penalized for starting a family.

In addition to her advocacy work, Felix has shown her entrepreneurial spirit through the launch of her footwear brand, Saysh. This brand, designed by women for women, is more than just a business venture—it's a statement about the importance of inclusivity and empowerment in sports and beyond. Through Saysh, Felix continues to inspire and uplift women, creating products that cater specifically to their needs and celebrating their unique strengths.

Felix's impact on the world of sports and society at large is profound. She has become a role model not only for young athletes but for anyone facing challenges in their pursuit of excellence. Her story is one of perseverance, integrity, and the courage to stand up for what is right, even in the face of adversity. As she navigated the highs and lows of her career, Felix has remained grounded, drawing strength from her family, her faith, and her unwavering belief in the power of hard work and determination.

As she steps into the next chapter of her life, Allyson Felix's legacy is secure. She leaves behind a lasting impact on the world of athletics, having redefined what it means to be an Olympian. Her influence will continue to be felt for generations to come, as she has not only set the standard for athletic excellence but also for using one's platform to advocate for change and uplift others.

Allyson Felix's journey is a powerful reminder that greatness is not just about winning medals; it's about how you use your success to make a difference in the world. Whether through her record-breaking performances on the track, her advocacy for women's rights, or her entrepreneurial endeavors, Felix has shown that true champions are those who inspire others, stand up for their beliefs, and leave the world better than they found it. As the most decorated U.S. track and field athlete in history, Allyson Felix's story will continue to inspire, motivate, and empower future generations to chase their dreams with the same passion, resilience, and grace that she has shown throughout her remarkable career.

Printed in Great Britain
by Amazon